Can Camels Dance?

Short Stories, Fuzzy Animals and Life Lessons

Karma for Kids Books

Norma MacDonald

Can Camels Dance?
Short Stories, Fuzzy Animals and Life Lessons

Copyright © 2018 Norma MacDonald

First Edition

Published by: Find Your Way Publishing, Inc.
PO BOX 667
Norway, ME 04268 U.S.A.
www.findyourwaypublishing.com

ISBN-13: 978-1-945290-15-2

ISBN-10: 1-945290-15-3

Library of Congress Control Number: 2018937490

Printed in the United States of America.

Dedication

This book is dedicated to all the people trying to make the world a better place. Keep going! You are making a positive difference!

"Never give up. You only get one life. Go for it!
Richard E. Grant

"Courage is not the absence of fear, but the triumph over it. The brave man is not he who does not feel afraid, but he who conquers that fear."
Nelson Mandela

Table of Contents

About This Book

Welcome to our Karma for Kids Book Series. We are very grateful that you picked up this book. We believe together we can make a positive difference, one child at a time. We strive to instill important life lessons in the lives of young children. We are firm believers that we reap what we sow and think that if this simple lesson is taught to children at a young age, their lives have the potential to be absolutely amazing.

We once knew a dog named Karma. She was a beautiful, Labrador retriever. It wasn't until after she passed, at 11 years old, that we realized just how fitting her name really was.

Karma is indeed a retriever.

Whatever we threw out, Karma was always happy to bring it back to us. It didn't matter what it was, she always brought it back. If we threw out an ugly, stinky, dirty sock she'd bring it back without question. If we threw out a sweet smelling, beautiful bouquet of flowers she'd bring it back. It's the same in life. Whatever you send out, is what you will get back, guaranteed, every time. Our Karma for Kids Book Series hopes to instill this easy-to-understand lesson into the lives of children at a young age. The Universe wants to happily bring you all that your heart desires, and it will, effortlessly. But first, you've got to throw out what you want it to bring back to you so that it can! Have fun with this and watch the magic happen. God bless!

Find all of Norma MacDonald's Karma for Kids Books at Amazon.com.

For more of our Karma for Kids books please visit us at:

www.karmaforkidsbooks.wordpress.com
or
www.findyourwaypublishing.com

Other books that we recommend to help children learn important life lessons:

Arctic Adventures: Short Stories, Fuzzy Animals, and Life Lessons by Norma MacDonald

Kyle Kitten and Friends: Short Stories, Fuzzy Animals, and Life Lessons by Norma MacDonald

The Panda Family Relies on Each Other: Short Stories, Fuzzy Animals, and Life Lessons by Norma MacDonald

Matt the African Meerkat and Friends: Short Stories, Fuzzy Animals, and Life Lessons by Norma MacDonald

Kimmie Koala and Friends: Short Stories, Fuzzy Animals, and Life Lessons by Norma MacDonald

Cranky Crocodile Saves the Day: Short Stories, Fuzzy Animals, and Life Lessons by Norma MacDonald

The Many Adventures of Peppy the Emperor Penguin: Short Stories, Fuzzy Animals, and Life Lessons by Norma MacDonald

Lucy Llama and Friends: Short Stories, Fuzzy Animals, and Life Lessons by Norma MacDonald

Ethan Eagle and Friends: Short Stories, Fuzzy Animals, and Life Lessons by Norma MacDonald

Billy Brown Bear and Friends: Short Stories, Fuzzy Animals, and Life Lessons by Norma MacDonald

Humble Heron and Friends: Short Stories, Fuzzy Animals, and Life Lessons by Norma MacDonald

Peter Penguin and Friends: Short Stories, Fuzzy Animals and Life Lessons by Norma MacDonald

Guaranteed Success for Kindergarten; 50 Easy Things You Can Do Today! by Marrae Kimball

Guaranteed Success for Grade School; 50 Easy Things You Can Do Today! by Marrae Kimball

The Secret Combination to Middle School: Real Advice from Real Kids, Ideas for Success, and Much More! by Marrae Kimball

Can Camels Dance?

Short Stories, Fuzzy Animals, and Life Lessons

Karma for Kids Books

Norma MacDonald

Chapter One

Every year, in July, a bunch of different kinds of animals from all over the huge Sahara desert gather at the Lakes of Ounianga for a very exciting event. The Lakes of Ounianga are part of a beautiful oasis in Northern Africa that has been around for thousands of years. The Sahara is the world's largest hot desert and is one of the hardest places to live on the planet. Some of the animals travel across the dry, hot desert for days and days to get to the oasis. Other animals walk for weeks and weeks before they spot the tall palm trees and red sand that surround the rolling hills and deep blue lakes of this amazing place.

Deserts are usually very, very dry. But an oasis is a special place in the desert that has lots of water and trees. The Lakes of Ounianga are the perfect place for the annual Saharan Animal Talent Competition. Many gather to compete, but many more come to watch and enjoy this great event. Many groups of desert animals spend months and months practicing for this special competition. This year, six different animal groups from all over the Sahara have been chosen to perform and compete. The groups include the red-necked ostriches, the spotty cheetahs, the Arabian camels, the monitor lizards, the African wild dogs, and the smallest animals of all, the hyrax.

By the time the animals who will take part in the competition arrive at the Lakes of Ounianga, they are very tired and hungry and just want to relax under a palm tree and have a good, long rest. This is especially true of the group of red-necked ostriches. For months and months, the group of six huge birds have been working super hard on their synchronized dance routine. Synchronized means that all of the birds do the same exact moves at the same exact time. Their long legs must do dance steps that match and are done together, at the same time as everyone else. The dance steps also have to fall to the beat of the rhythm of the drums that are part of the routine. The ostriches have the routine all together, most of the time. The only problem is Akila.

Akila is the youngest in the group and if she wasn't such a great dancer, the others would never have let her become a part of their dance troupe. Akila loves to dance, but she has one huge weakness—a lack of self-control. The other birds have talked to her, begged her, and threatened her about her crazy dance moves. But sometimes in the middle of their routine, Akila just can't stop herself from busting out into a whirling dance of her own.

It had been three weeks since Akila's last outburst. Her dance mates threaten to go to the Lakes of Ounianga without her. Akila promises to control herself and never again break away and dance any wild steps on her own. The ostriches vote on it and decide to keep her in the group. They want to give her another chance, and besides, they don't have time to replace her and train another ostrich before the competition.

Akila truly believes that she can control her urges. But the truth is she doesn't know how. It's like her big, two-toed feet have a mind of their own.

Her dance mates offer advice on how to control herself.

"The first thing you must do is admit that you sometimes have a problem with self-control."

Akila knows it's true. She has no problem admitting it.

"What makes you do all those wild dance moves?" her dance leader asks. "Maybe if you can figure out why it happens, you can stop it from happening. What do you think is the reason?"

Akila's answer is simple. "My feet just take off on their own."

"Can't you tell your feet they can do their own thing later? After our synchronized routine is finished?"

"I've tried that. Sometimes it works, sometimes it doesn't."

Akila is stuck. She doesn't know what to do about her problem. She hopes that she can make it through the rehearsals and the performance without anything bad happening. But she has her doubts.

The next day, the group is all rested up and ready to start practicing on the giant stage that has been set up between two of the biggest, bluest lakes. A gentle breeze blows and waves the palm fronds of the trees that surround the stage.

As the drums start beating softly, the six ostriches form a circle and dip their heads up and down with the rhythm. Akila's dance mates give her a warning look and she smiles in return. She can do this. She knows she can. Her feet will not betray her this time.

The dance routine is going great, as the giant birds step and bob their heads in unison. The drums beat their rhythm stronger and stronger, as they dance together perfectly. They are close to the end of the dance and so far, Akila is right in sync with the others.

But then, all of a sudden, her feet begin to itch and twitch.

Akila tries her best to ignore the feeling in her toes.

Much to her horror, her feet begin to tap out their own rhythm. The other dancers stare down at those rebellious toes with shock and fear. There's nothing they can do to stop what is about to happen.

Akila bursts into the center of the group and performs a wild and unique rhythmic dance, all by herself.

The dance itself is great; Akila is a terrific dancer, but it's not part of the routine.

Her dance mates look at each other horrified! It is only one day until the competition and she is ruining everything. The six ostriches leave the stage in silence. Akila's sinks down in shame. When they get to a private place, she bursts into tears. "I am so sorry. I just can't control myself. When I hear the music, sometimes my feet just start to do their own thing for a little bit. It usually doesn't last long." She sniffs and sniffles. Her dance mates wag their heads back and forth. "What are we going to do?" they ask.

The leader of their group thinks about it for a couple of minutes. All of a sudden, her black eyes brighten. She wonders why she didn't think of it earlier. "I knew it! My mom often says that there is always a solution to every problem. You just have to stop and think. Why don't we just make Akila's wild dancing part of the routine?" she asks.

The ostriches nod their heads. "Great idea. It's worth a shot." They all turn and look at Akila. Her face beams with happiness.

"But it can only happen once. And only for one minute," says the dance leader.

Akila agrees. "I promise. Just once. I think if I can at least have a chance to let loose, at least once, then I will be good to go. Thanks everyone!"

The ostrich dance group trusts that Akila will try her best.

"There is a solution to every problem," the dance leader said optimistically, "and I'm glad we came up with a plan as a team."

Chapter Two

Cheetahs are one of the fastest animals on earth. They can run 60 miles per hour. That's fast! The fastest human on earth can only run about 28 miles per hour. So if humans try to race cheetahs, the humans are left in the dust.

The Northwest African Cheetahs are big cats with mostly white fur covered with black spots that fade to brown on their strong legs. Most cheetahs have dark stripes that run down from the corners of their eyes making it look like trails of tears. But this doesn't mean that they are crying.

Casimir is not the fastest runner in his family, but he is the most handsome Cheetah in all of the Sahara desert. And he knows it. Not only is he good-looking, but he also has a beautiful, deep singing voice. Because of his physical beauty and his rich voice, all the young cheetah girls are always swarming around him and he loves their attention.

Before he starts off for his long journey to the Lakes of Ounianga, the animals in Casimir's home village throw a huge going away party for him. All night long they sing and dance and eat heaps and heaps of food. They all believe Casimir will win the Saharan Animal Talent Competition for being best singer of the Sahara. Casimir believes it, too.

Before he goes to bed, his grandmother pulls him aside to speak with him. "My dear boy," she says. "I fear you have too much pride. Too much pride can lead to your downfall. Be careful."

Casimir just laughs it off. "Don't worry, Granny. A little pride is a good thing. I'll be just fine."

"Yes, a little pride is a good thing," his grandmother lovingly said, "but humility is a good thing, too. Humility is thinking as highly of others as you do yourself. Humility is not thinking you are better than everyone else. Sometimes when we think we are better than others, life will give us a hard lesson proving otherwise."

"I'll keep that in mind, Granny. Thanks."

A huge group of animals come to wish Casimir farewell. They clap and cheer him on as he starts his long walk northward towards the Lakes of Ounianga. A group of his cheetah friends burst out running together ahead of him as a way of showing their support for his long journey. He loves the attention and trots off feeling very, very important and happy.

The trip takes him a few weeks. He hunts along the way and sleeps in trees. Every night Casimir sings his love songs. Loads of night animals gather around to listen to him. When he stops singing, the animals ask him to continue. "Everybody loves my voice," he says to himself. As he falls asleep, he imagines what it will be like when he receives the singer's special crown at the Saharan Animal Talent Competition. In his mind, he can hear the cheers and can see the admiring eyes of all of the animals of Northern Africa.

One thing about deserts is that they are very dry. It can be very hard to find good water to drink. Casimir has never made this trip north, but plenty of friends had warned him about how important it would be to know how to find water. He had only listened with one ear. Now he wishes he had paid more attention and asked more questions. Quite a while has passed since he's had his last drink and his throat feels dry and scratchy. Some of the water he finds is not very tasty. After a few days like this, he starts to worry. "What if there's no water to drink. I could die of thirst!"

One night as he is resting in a large tree, Casimir opens his mouth to sing. The voice that comes out is hoarse and very off key. He clears his throat and tries again. No change. "Maybe I just need a good, long drink of fresh water. That must be it," he says to himself. "Once I get to the Lakes of Ounianga, everything will be just fine."

But water gets harder and harder to find. By the time Casimir reaches the oasis, he can barely talk above a whisper. "I need water. Water.

Quickly. Someone bring me some water," he cries in his crackly voice.

Those who work to organize the competition are ready with water and other refreshments and a cool place in the shade for those who have made the long journey through the Sahara desert. Casimir accepts their help. After drinking quite a bit of clean, cool water, he curls up in a tall tree in a breezy spot by one of the lakes and takes a long, peaceful nap.

Casimir wakes up to the sound of a voice more beautiful than anything he has ever heard. He looks around but cannot figure out where the singing is coming from. At first he thinks it's his imagination. But the voice grows louder and rises higher. And then suddenly it stops. Is this the voice of one of his competitors?

The cheetah climbs down from the tree, clears his throat, and prepares to sing his favorite song. He will show the other singers that they have no chance of winning.

But when he opens his mouth, a mere squeak comes out. He hums a bit and then tries again. Same thing. Just a pitiful squeak. He needs to find a doctor, right away.

The doctor looks down Casimir's throat and shakes his head. "Your voice needs rest. If you do not talk or sing for the next week, maybe your voice will return to normal."

"A week?!" cries Casimir. "But the competition is in five days."

"Shhhh," says the doctor. "Don't talk. Follow my advice and maybe, just maybe, you will be able to sing in the competition."

Casimir slinks away from the doctor feeling disappointment and worry in his heart. He hopes his voice heals and returns for the competition.

Chapter Three

The one-humped Arabian camel, also called a Dromedary, has a unique way of walking. Unlike most animals, camels move both legs on one side of the body at the same time. And unlike most other animals, they can walk for about 100 miles without having a drop of water to drink. How can they do that?

The secret lies in the camel's hump. The Arabian camels store a great gob of fat in those humps of theirs. When the camels need it, the fat changes into water and energy. And when they are able to stop for a drink, they really load up!

The group of ten Arabian camels moves across the hot desert at a steady pace. They are on their way to compete as dancers at the Saharan Animal Talent Competition. Like all the other competitors, these camels have trained for months and months. Five of them are girls, five of them are boys. Their dance is very tricky. With their long legs, they must weave in and out and around each other without bumping into each other.

At one point in the dance, the camels all kneel down on their front knees, but then have to rise up together, at the same time. Getting up from the knees is no easy thing for a camel. This part of the slow dance has been a problem. Babikir is the oldest member of their group and he always watches the others and has a habit of pointing out their mistakes. But if any of the other camels point out his mistakes, he gets very upset and defensive. "I've been doing this traditional dance longer than any of you. I am a pro and know best how it should be done."

Every evening as the hot red sun dips down into the horizon, the camels gather for a practice session. The youngest girl camel struggles and struggles to get the steps just right. She needs more practice because it seems like no matter how hard she tries she just can't get the steps right. Babikir yells at her, which makes tears well up in her eyes.

"Stop that crying," says Babikir. "If you would pay more attention to your feet I wouldn't have to correct you all the time. Now pay attention."

"I'll try," the young camel sniffles. "I'll try."

Babikir grunts. "Try harder."

The camels wake up before sunrise each morning. Babikir doesn't believe in sleeping late. First thing in the morning, he leads the group with a morning stretch. "It keeps our bodies flexible," he says, as he moves his long neck up and down and from side to side. Though sleepy, the other camels imitate his movements.

"Not like that," Babikir says to a couple of the boy camels. "You should stretch like me." He wants them all to stretch and exercise in unison. Half of them want to do it on their own, but Babikir insists they do everything together, exactly like he does it. He likes to point out the others faults, even when they are just stretching.

"You would think we never do anything right," the camels mumble amongst themselves.

Babikir hears their grumbling. "Do you want to win the competition or not?" he asks. "I'm only trying to help."

"A word of encouragement every once in a while would help. Putting us down all the time only makes us mad and hurts our feelings." one camel says.

Another chimes in, "It would be helpful if you could say something positive once in a while. Haven't you heard that saying, you catch more flies with honey than vinegar? It means you get more by being kind and encouraging then by being mean and critical. "

Babikir disagrees. "We can't let ourselves get all puffed up, thinking there's no room for improvement," he says. "A little criticism never hurt anyone."

"A little criticism?" asks one of the camels. "I'd say the criticism has been non-stop. When was the last time you gave one of us a compliment? When was the last time you told us that we did a good job? We are not trying to complain but it does get frustrating when we continually try our best, and it's never enough for you. It seems like all you do is notice and point out our flaws."

Babikir ignores the comment and the questions all together. "Let's get going. We still have three more days before we arrive at the Lakes of Ounianga."

The journey to the oasis continues without any trouble. By the time they need water; they find a source that's able to take care of the needs of all ten camels. Arabian camels can drink up to 30 gallons of water in less than fifteen minutes! After they have all drank their fill, the camels find shade under a palm tree and sit down for a bit of a rest.

But Babikir is in a big hurry to get to the lakes. He doesn't want to waste any time. "Up, up, up!" he shouts. "We can rest when we get there. No time to be lazy."

"But we're tired," the camels say. "Can't we have just one hour of peace and rest?"

Babikir shakes his head. "No way. We do not have time for this. You need all the practice you can get. There's no time to rest. Let's go."

But the nine camels have had enough and refuse to get up. Babikir stomps around in anger, but the others don't pay him any attention. When they are good and ready, the nine camels get up and continue the last leg of their trip.

They arrive at the Lakes of Ounianga just as darkness falls. The sky twinkles with sparkling stars and the warm air is filled with the sound of music and singing. The camels set up their camp and settle in for a good night of rest. The next day is the rehearsal and they all want to be fresh and ready.

As usual, Babikir is the first one up in the morning, and awakens the rest of the group. After stretching, he wants to run through their dance routine a couple times before they head off to practice on the big stage. He is so focused on watching all the other camels' feet, that he doesn't watch his own step. He doesn't see the large dip in the sand. All of a sudden, his right front foot stumbles and snaps!

Babikir howls out in pain. The other camels gather around him. "Can you move it?" they ask. "Do you think it's broken?"

"I don't know," he says. "Go find a doctor."

Two of the camels race off to get help while the rest of the camels stay and comfort Babikir. "Don't worry. It's probably just sprained."

They were right. It was a sprain. The doctor gave Babikir a shot to reduce the swelling and told him not to put pressure on it for at least 24 hours.

"But I have to dance tonight!" Babikir cries.

The doctor shakes his head. "Not tonight. You need to rest it for a few days if you want to compete this weekend."

Babikir groans. "Why didn't I keep my eyes on my own dancing?" he asks himself. Now he is unsure of whether or not he will be able to dance during the competition. From this point on, Babikir decides he will pay more attention to his own self, rather than focusing on what everyone else is doing. He will try to rest and be more positive. He makes a mental note to try to see the best in others, because being critical doesn't help anything.

Chapter Four

Arafa is a lovely monitor lizard with dark stripes across her brown back and tail. Monitor lizards are smaller than alligators, but longer than a broom handle. Arafa is a desert monitor lizard and she spends most of her life hibernating. She and her family are mostly active between the months of May and July, but the rest of the time they sleep a lot.

Every June, the desert monitor lizards hold a singing competition. The winner gets to travel to the Lakes of Ounianga to compete in the Saharan

Animal Talent Competition held every July. This year, the competition amongst the lizards is really tough. There are five monitor lizards, three girls and two boys, who all have beautiful voices. No one knows who will be the winner.

Arafa comes from a family of talented singers. Three years earlier, Arafa's older sister won the singing competition amongst the monitor lizards. When she competed in the Saharan Animal Talent Competition, she came in second place, which was really special. But ever since then, Arafa has dreamed of going to the Saharan Animal Talent Competition and winning the first place crown.

Arafa's family is very supportive of her goal. They do many things for her, like hunting and other daily chores, so she can focus her time and energy on training her voice. But sometimes Arafa expects way too much from them. She has very specific tastes when it comes to food. "I know that if I eat those tasty little bird eggs, they will make my voice stronger. You want me to win, right?" she says to her younger brothers and sisters. And so they work extra hard to bring her all the things she wants. But it's never enough. There's always something Arafa wants her family to do for her.

"My feet and tail are really aching," she says to her little sister. "Please rub them for me?"

Her younger sister sighs. "I did that for you yesterday, and the day before. Can't I have a day off?"

Arafa gives her a hurt look. "Don't you want to help me become the best singer in all of Saharan Africa?" she asks.

"Of course I do," says her sister.

Arafa extends her feet and tail towards her. "Please. It's important to me. Just for a half an hour, ok?"

Her younger sister sighs again, but goes ahead and rubs Arafa's tail and feet.

When Arafa is sleeping, her whole family gets together to talk about the situation. "She's become so selfish," her oldest brother complains. "And if she wins this competition and heads off to the Lakes of Ounianga, it will only get worse."

All Arafa's brothers and sisters nod in agreement. "And she seems to want a lot of things lately."

"It's only two days until the competition," says their mother. "Let's see if she wins. And if she does, we can have another family discussion, including Arafa. Please, let's just do what we can to support her for now. We'll talk about this again after the competition."

Arafa's family all agree to follow their mother's advice, but they are not happy about it. They keep on doing whatever she asks, which becomes more and more, the closer they get to the night of the competition.

That evening, when Arafa takes the stage and sings better than they've ever heard her sing before, the family is filled with joy. The crowd claps and cheers louder and longer for Arafa than for any of the other singers. Arafa wins the monitor lizard competition!

The next day, the monitor lizards throw a big congratulations party for Arafa and invite all the animals from miles around. When the party is over, the family heads home and sit down to have their discussion with Arafa about her upcoming trip to the Lakes of Ounianga.

After the family decides who will travel together with Arafa and who will stay home, they talk about what they can reasonably do to support Arafa.

"I need at least five of you to come along and take care of things for me," Arafa says.

"Five? One of us should be enough," says her older brother.

Arafa pouts and whines and finally, her parents decide that her mother and one brother and one sister will go with her to the competition at the Lakes of Ounianga.

Arafa packs six big and heavy bags.

"I'm not going to carry those," says her brother.

"Me either," says her sister.

Arafa pleads and cries to her mother, "But I need all these things if I'm going to have any chance of winning the competition."

Her mother shakes her head. "What you need is a beautiful voice. And you already have that. You can bring one bag. And make sure it's not too heavy."

Arafa stomps and pouts, but she can see that her mother will not change her mind. An hour later, they're on their way. They don't have far to go, just a day and a half of travelling. But Arafa wants to go slow so she doesn't get tired out. It takes them two full days instead. By the time they arrive, her mother and brother and sister are exhausted. But

Arafa insists that they go find food for her and a better place to sleep because the area they were given is too noisy for her. "If I don't get good rest, I won't win," she says. "And when you come back, I need you to rub my feet. They are really sore."

Her brother and sister have had enough. "We quit. We have been slaving for you for weeks and now we are going to go enjoy ourselves," they say.

Arafa is left with her mother. "How can they be so selfish?" she asks. "Make them come back. Make one of them rub my feet, please."

But Arafa's mother just shakes her head. "Let them go, Arafa. You have received heaps of help already and they feel like you're taking advantage of them. Maybe you are the one who is being selfish. Life is about give and take. You can't just take all of the time. I think you are getting accustomed to their kindness and just keep expecting more and more from them."

Arafa frowns. "Don't they want me to win?"

"Of course they do," says her mother. "But they are not your slaves. I think you need to start taking care of some of your own needs. I will do what I can to help, but you can't ask for so much. Maybe you should stop and think before you request something and ask yourself if you can do it yourself. And while you are at it, maybe you should ask yourself what you can do to help others from time to time."

Arafa puts her head down and sulks. How is she going to win if she has to take care of everything herself? "So unfair," she grumbles. "But I guess I see what you are saying. Maybe I have started to take advantage of their kindness. I just thought everyone wanted to help and I have gotten use to it. Now I can see that everyone is starting to get upset so, I am glad that you brought it to my attention. I don't want to be selfish. Thank you, mother, I will try to do better." Although an uncomfortable subject, Arafa is happy that she now knows what she can do to make it better. The first thing she is going to do is soak her feet and think about how she can help her family more.

Chapter Five

This group of African wild dogs have been singing together since they were pups. From early on, everyone knew they had great talent and would someday make a great name for themselves. That day has come and the dogs have been practicing for months and months to get everything just right. But there's one problem. Every time a change is made, Moussa, the youngest member of the group, has a hard time adjusting.

Moussa eats the same things every day. He sleeps in the same place, wakes at the same time, and goes to bed at the same hour every night. He really likes to have a regular routine.

It's the same with his singing. Moussa likes to know what is expected of him and doesn't like anything to change. Once he learns a new song, he sings it over and over and over again until he gets it just right. But if the group wants to make an adjustment to one of the words or one of the notes, Moussa panics. He is afraid he will forget the change or do it wrong.

The other dogs are constantly reassuring Moussa. "You will be just fine. We trust you. You are a great singer. Try not to worry."

But Moussa worries. He worries a lot. As the day gets closer for the group to make the journey to the Lakes of Ounianga for the competition, Moussa worries more and more and more. How is he going to be able to sleep in a different place? Will they have the food he's used to eating? Will he be able to wake up at the same time?

The morning they are to leave, Moussa stays in bed and think and thinks and thinks about the trip. He is so worried that he decides he cannot make the journey to the competition. The group will just have to manage without him. He gets up and goes to find the other dogs to let them know what he has decided. He is not going to go.

"There you are," they say when they see him. "We have been waiting and waiting. Where is your bag?"

Moussa bows his head down. "I don't have one. I have decided to stay home. I think you will be better off without me."

The other members of his group are shocked. They circle around him and try to reassure him. "No. No. No, Moussa. We need you. The group won't be the same without you. You must come!"

Moussa shakes his head. "I don't think I can do it."

"We think that you can, Moussa. What can we do to help?" they ask.

"I don't know," says Moussa. "I'm just worried."

"We will support you," the other dogs say, patting him on the back. "Don't worry. We will try to keep a good routine and make as few changes as possible. Do you think you can at least try?"

Moussa thinks about it for a couple minutes. He doesn't want to let his group down. Maybe if the journey is calm and there aren't any big changes…maybe he can do it. Maybe. "Okay, I'll try," he says.

"Hooray!" the group shouts. They quickly go help Moussa pack his bag. Fifteen minutes later they are headed toward the Lakes of Ounianga; a journey that will take them three days.

Knowing Moussa's anxiety, the wild dogs do their best to make the journey as easy as possible for the youngest member of their group. They get up at the same time every day, make sure Moussa gets his favorite foods, and snuggle together to sleep as soon as the stars fill the night sky.

Moussa appreciates everything they do for him. "I think I am going to be all right," he says to himself as he falls asleep each night.

The wild African dogs arrive at the Lakes of Ounianga the day of the rehearsal. When Moussa sees the huge stage, he trembles. "I'm not used to singing up on a high platform like that," he says. "I don't think I can sing if I am up so high. The stage at home is only a foot off the ground. That one is as high as the heavens."

The other dogs talk to Moussa in soothing voices. "The stage is not that high. Wait until later when we actually have our rehearsal. You'll be just fine. Just wait and see. At least give it a try."

But Moussa has a sick feeling in his stomach. He's not sure he can handle this change. Later, when it is time for the rehearsal, Moussa steps up onto the stage with his group. His legs tremble and his heart races, but after a few minutes, he realizes it's not as scary as he thought it would be. Maybe he can do this.

The African wild dogs sing their song beautifully. But when they finish, the director of the competition pulls them aside. "I'm sorry. But your song is 15 seconds too long. You're going to need to shorten it up a little."

"No problem," say the dogs. "We'll take care of that."

But Moussa panics. "Change the song? But the competition is tomorrow. It's too late to make changes. I won't be able to remember and I'll mess everything up."

Although his fellow singers tell him it'll be fine, they have plenty of time to practice, Moussa is super scared. Will he be able to make the adjustment?

"Moussa, you can do this," say the dogs. "You didn't think you'd be able to make the trip, but you faced your fears and you did great. You didn't think you'd be able to get up on the big stage because you had never done it before, but you found your courage and you gave it a try, and again, you succeeded. You will succeed at this, too. Stop worrying so much. It is good to go out of your comfort zone from time to time. Now let's go, we will figure it out together."

Moussa took a deep breath, "Wow, I guess you're right. It just feels scary."

"Change can be scary, but most of the time, change is a good thing."

"Okay, let's go practice so we can will this competition!" Moussa exclaimed excitedly. "It might feel a little scary, but it will be worth it in the end."

Chapter Six

The Hyrax dancers are the last group of competitors to arrive at the Lakes of Ounianga. The Hyrax are small furry animals that live in rock crevices. They always hang out in large groups. Their journey across the Saharan desert was long and hard and filled with danger, mostly because they are small and are hunted by other desert animals. But despite the troubles, the Hyrax arrive just in time. Fifty of their family members have come to the competition to cheer them on.

The Hyrax dance is fast and swirling with lots of acrobatics. The small animals use little trampolines to jump and toss each other into the air. Their routine is very unique. Like many of the other talented animals at the competition, the Hyrax have trained since they were itty bitty. Their dance routine is spectacular and many believe the Hyrax will be the winners of the dance part of the Saharan Animal Talent Competition.

Fadoul is one of the six Hyrax dancers. She is a great dancer, but she has one big problem. Fadoul is messy. Back home, her mother always has to remind her to clean her room, wash her face, and brush her hair. When she eats, she often spills food on herself and then forgets to clean it off.

Fadoul's dance group is constantly checking her to make sure she is clean and tidy. They know the judges will not only make their decision on how the groups and individuals perform, but on how they look, as well. One messy Hyrax can spoil the appearance of the entire group and cost the victory. The other Hyrax have lots to do to get ready. But as they prepare for the competition, the group leader gives a repeated warning. "Before we go on stage, make sure we check Fadoul."

When the day of the competition arrives the singers and dancers are jumpy and nervous. They spend the hours before the competition practicing and getting ready for their big night which begins at sunset. During the day, the animals find out the order in which they will perform. The information is posted and everyone gathers around. First on the list is a group of dancing gazelles. No one really wants to be first, so all the other performers are relieved it's not them.

An hour before the performance, the animals seek a quiet place alone so they can focus on the performance that lies ahead.

Akila the Red-necked Ostrich sits under a tree and thinks about the promise she made to her group. She will control her feet. She will limit her wild dancing to one minute. She reminds herself over and over again that she can do this.

Casimir the Cheetah has been resting his voice for the past five days. An hour before the competition, he sits at the breezy shore of one of the lakes and begins his voice warming routine. Slowly he lets out the sounds. His voice seems to have recovered. Casimir is thrilled. Several young cheetah girls sit nearby and smile at him as he goes through his voice exercises. His confidence returns. Once again, Casimir is convinced in his heart that there is no other singer in the whole world who is better than he is.

Babikir the Arabian Camel has been staying off his injured foot and has tried hard to think positive thoughts about the evening's performance. The night before, he wasn't able to join his team for the rehearsal, but from the audience he watched the other camels dance. Rather than being critical, he offered positive comments to his dance mates. Now, an hour before the competition begins, Babikir is rehearsing the dance routine in his mind. He still isn't sure if his foot is strong enough to dance, but he is going to give it his best shot.

Arafa the Monitor Lizard rests on a small hill across from the giant stage. She still thinks it's a bit unfair that her family members refuse to take care of all her needs. But when she tries to put herself in their shoes, she understands. If one of her siblings were demanding that she do everything for them when they could do it themselves, she'd probably get frustrated, too. Arafa imagines how it will be when she has won the competition. Everyone will be excited. She hopes her winning will be somewhat of a thank you to them for all they've done for her.

An hour before the competition begins; Moussa is pacing back and forth behind the giant stage. Even though the group has run through the changes they made to their song at least a dozen times, Moussa still worries. Will he remember the changes? He sings the song over and over and over to himself. He tries really hard to think positive thoughts. But the fear of failure keeps coming back. He can't make it go away.

Fadoul the Hyrax took a little swim in one of the emerald lakes and is drying off on a warm rock.

Her fur is all clean. Now if she can just stay clean for the next hour, everyone will be happy.

As the fiery sun begins to drop down on this lovely desert oasis, the singers and dancers of the Saharan desert make their final preparations for this very special night. The judges are ready and set to go. All the competitors wait in a large area behind the giant stage. The animals jiggle and wiggle as they are all quite jittery with nerves. This is the night they have been preparing so long for; some for weeks and others for years.

The warm, dry air crackles with excitement. The groups of dancers make up the first part of the competition, then there is an intermission, and then the singers will take the stage. At the end of it all, the winners will be announced. The first up are the dancing gazelles.

The graceful gazelles whirl and twirl in a lovely ballet routine. Unfortunately, towards the very end of the dance, one of the gazelles trips and knocks into one of the other dancers and they both stumble and fall. The crowd gasps. Such a bad start to the competition makes all of those waiting backstage even more nervous. But they gracefully finished their routine.

After the gazelles finishing came the big moment for the Red-necked Ostriches to dance. Akila, and the rest of her group, take a few deep breaths to relax, and then with confidence, take the stage. But Akila isn't feeling very confident. She is very nervous. But remembering her promise, she does everything she can to dance in step with the other ostriches.

Not ten seconds into the performance, Akila feels that familiar twitch in her feet. "No. No. No," she says to herself. "It's not time. Not yet." If she can just control her feet to dance in harmony with the rest of the group until the drum beat signal comes, all will be well.

Akila fights hard and just when she thinks she cannot control her feet a second more, the drummer changes the beat and it's time for Akila to move to the center of the stage and do her own wild dance.

What freedom she feels as she lets loose and dances around the stage. Her feet do their own thing to the fast beat of the drums. The crowd hoots and hollers with excitement. Akila feels happier than she has ever felt in her life. But then the drummer changes the beat. Can Akila gain control over herself and rejoin her fellow dancers to finish together? "I can do this," she says. "I can."

And she does. The Red-necked Ostriches step to the music together in a beautiful ending. The crowd cheers. The judges give very high scores. Will the ostriches be the winners? They will have to wait and see. There are still many other dance acts to come.

Backstage, Babikir the Arabian camel practices his dance steps. His foot is sore, but he believes he can dance. One of his dance mates struggles with one of the complicated steps, but rather than being negative Babikir says, "Don't worry. You'll do great." His dance mate smiles warmly. She's so glad that Babikir is learning to be less critical.

The Arabian camels take the stage and even though Babikir stumbles a few times, their dance goes well. The crowd enjoys it. The judges didn't give them as high a score as they would have liked, but overall they were happy with the results. Well, most of them. Babikir felt sad that his injury kept them from winning, but his group encourages him. "Don't be disappointed, Babikir. We didn't quit! We came out here and did our best."

Babikir thanks them. In the future, he will work hard to build others up with positive words.

Next up are the Hyrax dancers. Backstage, Fadoul looks at herself very carefully in the mirror. Her fur is clean and smooth. She is ready. All the members of her group nod their heads in approval.

The small furry animals dance their little hearts out, jumping, tumbling, and whirling around the stage. They get the loudest cheers of all, mostly because so many of their friends and family came to watch the competition. The judges give them very high scores. They leave the stage with great big smiles on their little faces.

After a brief intermission, the time has come for the singing part of the competition. Some really great solo singers and wonderful singing groups are eager to perform.

The group singers are first up. Moussa, the African wild dog, paces back and forth as he waits for his group to take the stage. Will he remember the changes that have been made to the song?

The African wild dogs take the stage and begin to sing their beautiful song filled with rich harmony. Moussa opens his mouth wide. The words and melody flow out from his heart. He has no trouble remembering. The crowd and the judges love the African wild dogs. Moussa leaves the stage in high spirits.

After two more group acts, the moment arrives for the soloists. Both Arafa, the Monitor Lizard, and Casimir, the Saharan Cheetah, have a great chance of winning the competition.

Casimir is certain that he will be the winner, and tells Arafa that he is sorry in advance that she is going to lose to him. He has no doubt that the crowd and judges will see that he is the greatest singer in the Sahara. Arafa is hurt but wishes him good luck anyway. "I just want to share my voice and song with others," she says, "If it uplifts someone I will be happy." Casimir shrugs his shoulders and struts onto the stage. He approaches the microphone without a hint of fear. He knows he is the best of the best. The music starts and he fills his lungs, ready to belt out the first note of his love song. But when that first note comes out, it's not what he thinks it will be. Instead, a loud croak, like that of a sick toad bursts out of his mouth. The crowd gasps in surprise. Casimir can't believe his ears and is very embarrassed. He barely finishes the song, then dashes off the stage and searches for a place to hide. He remembered what his grandmother said about the tough lessons we sometimes learn when we think we are better than others. He wished he hadn't acted so conceited. Now he knew that there were others who could sing just as good as and even better than he could. He feels anxious to apologize to his grandmother and especially to Arafa for the way he acted.

The last singer of the night is Arafa the Monitor Lizard. Her beautiful voice brings the crowd to its feet as they roar with applause. The judges have nothing but praise. Everyone knows she will be crowned the winner. When the announcement is made, Arafa gives a lovely speech.

"I want to give a huge thanks to my family. They have been extremely supportive and have taught me a most important lesson. Others can help us on our journey, but we must also help ourselves. And not forget to help others as well.

A group of Grey Crowned cranes win the dance competition and the group singing prize is won by a trio of Colobus monkeys. When the competition is over, all the animals gather for a huge feast to celebrate together. They are all happy for each other. It was a great competition and everyone looks forward to the next one.

Will You Help Us Out?

Would you please consider leaving reviews for our books? They don't have to be long and will only take a minute. It would mean a lot and help us get the word out, to other children, as well. Thank you so much! We are extremely grateful.

AFTERWORD

Thanks again for picking up this book! You are participating in making our world a better place to live and grow. When children learn that they will always get back what they give, they will start to navigate their lives in incredible ways. When you give a smile, and make someone's heart feel lighter and happier, because of it, you can be sure that you will receive something in the near future that will make your heart happier as well. When you do something kind for someone, you can be sure that someone will do something kind for you in the coming days ahead. It is truly amazing how it works! Have fun with it and enjoy!

For more of our *Karma for Kids Books* please visit us at:

www.karmaforkidsbooks.wordpress.com
or
www.findyourwaypublishing.com

Find Norma MacDonald and her books online at Amazon.com.

Arctic Adventures: Short Stories, Fuzzy Animals, and Life Lessons

Kyle Kitten and Friends: Short Stories, Fuzzy Animals, and Life Lessons

The Panda Family Relies on Each Other: Short Stories, Fuzzy Animals, and Life Lessons

Matt the African Meerkat and Friends: Short Stories, Fuzzy Animals, and Life Lessons

The Many Adventures of Peppy the Emperor Penguin: Short Stories, Fuzzy Animals, and Life Lessons
Kimmie Koala and Friends: Short Stories, Fuzzy Animals, and Life Lessons

Cranky Crocodile Saves the Day: Short Stories, Fuzzy Animals, and Life Lessons

Lucy Llama and Friends: Short Stories, Fuzzy Animals, and Life Lessons

Ethan the Eagle and Friends; Short Stories, Fuzzy Animals, and Life Lessons

Billy Brown Bear and Friends; Short Stories, Fuzzy Animals, and Life Lessons

Humble Heron and Friends; Short Stories, Fuzzy Animals, and Life Lessons

Peter Penguin and Friends; Short Stories, Fuzzy Animals, and Life Lessons

Other books that we recommend to help children learn important life lessons:

Guaranteed Success for Kindergarten; 50 Easy Things You Can Do Today! by Marrae Kimball

Guaranteed Success for Grade School; 50 Easy Things You Can Do Today! by Marrae Kimball

The Secret Combination to Middle School: Real Advice from Real Kids, Ideas for Success, and Much More! by Marrae Kimball

High School Success: How to Create Your Own Path, Beat Anxiety & Depression, Master Your Goals & Dreams by Marrae Kimball

Again, thank you for reading and sharing this book! YOU are making the world a better place. Please consider leaving a short review as it helps us spread the message! Children deserve the very best that life has to offer.

All children deserve a chance at a successful and happy life.

If you have ideas for stories, please feel free to share and send them to:

Melissa Eshleman
Find Your Way Publishing, Inc.
PO Box 667
Norway, ME 04268
Melissa@findyourwaypublishing.com

www.findyourwaypublishing.com

Thank you!

Disclaimer

The purpose of this book is for entertainment purposes only. This book is designed to provide information and motivation to our readers. The content of each story is the sole expression and opinion of its author, and not necessarily that of the publisher. Names, characters, businesses, places, and incidents are either the products of the authors' imaginations or used in a fictitious manner. Any resemblance to actual persons, living or dead, businesses, companies, events, locales, or actual events is entirely coincidental. This book is not intended nor is it implied to be a substitute for professional medical advice, and any medical advice and any medical information contained in this book is not intended to be diagnostic or treatment in any way. The author and publisher are not engaged in rendering medical, psychological, legal, or any other professional services. If medical, psychological or other expert assistance is required, please talk to your physician and locate the services of a competent professional. The author and publisher shall have neither liability nor responsibility to any person or entity with respect to any loss or damage caused, or alleged to have been caused, directly or indirectly, by the information contained in this book. Neither the publisher nor the individual author(s) shall be liable for any physical, psychological, emotional, financial, or commercial damages, including, but not limited to, special, incidental, consequential or other damages. If you do not wish to be bound by the above, you may return this book along with a copy of the receipt to the publisher for a full refund.